'The color is hideous enough, and unreliable enough, and infuriating enough, but the pattern is torturing . . .'

CHARLOTTE PERKINS GILMAN
Born 1860, New England, USA
Died 1935, California, USA

'The Yellow Wall-Paper' was first published in 1892; 'The Rocking-Chair' in 1893; and 'Old Water' in 1911.

GILMAN IN PENGUIN CLASSICS
The Yellow Wall-Paper, Herland and Selected Writings

CHARLOTTE PERKINS GILMAN

The Yellow Wall-Paper

PENGUIN BOOKS

PENGUIN CLASSICS

UK | USA | Canada | Ireland | Australia
India | New Zealand | South Africa

Penguin Books is part of the Penguin Random House group of companies
whose addresses can be found at global.penguinrandomhouse.com.

This selection published in Penguin Classics 2015

013

Set in 9.5/13 pt Baskerville 10 Pro
Typeset by Jouve (UK), Milton Keynes
Printed in Great Britain by Clays Ltd, Elcograf S.p.A.

A CIP catalogue record for this book is available from the British Library

ISBN: 978-0-141-39741-2

www.greenpenguin.co.uk

MIX
Paper from
responsible sources
FSC® C018179

Penguin Random House is committed to a
sustainable future for our business, our readers
and our planet. This book is made from Forest
Stewardship Council® certified paper.

Contents

The Yellow Wall-Paper

It is very seldom that mere ordinary people like John and myself secure ancestral halls for the summer.

A colonial mansion, a hereditary estate, I would say a haunted house, and reach the height of romantic felicity – but that would be asking too much of fate!

Still I will proudly declare that there is something queer about it.

Else, why should it be let so cheaply? And why have stood so long untenanted?

John laughs at me, of course, but one expects that in marriage.

John is practical in the extreme. He has no patience with faith, an intense horror of superstition, and he scoffs openly at any talk of things not to be felt and seen and put down in figures.

John is a physician, and *perhaps* – (I would not say it to a living soul, of course, but this is dead paper and a great relief to my mind –) *perhaps* that is one reason I do not get well faster.

You see he does not believe I am sick!

And what can one do?

If a physician of high standing, and one's own husband,

assures friends and relatives that there is really nothing the matter with one but temporary nervous depression – a slight hysterical tendency – what is one to do?

My brother is also a physician, and also of high standing, and he says the same thing.

So I take phosphates or phosphites – whichever it is, and tonics, and journeys, and air, and exercise, and am absolutely forbidden to 'work' until I am well again.

Personally, I disagree with their ideas.

Personally, I believe that congenial work, with excitement and change, would do me good.

But what is one to do?

I did write for a while in spite of them; but it *does* exhaust me a good deal – having to be so sly about it, or else meet with heavy opposition.

I sometimes fancy that in my condition if I had less opposition and more society and stimulus – but John says the very worst thing I can do is to think about my condition, and I confess it always makes me feel bad.

So I will let it alone and talk about the house.

The most beautiful place! It is quite alone, standing well back from the road, quite three miles from the village. It makes me think of English places that you read about, for there are hedges and walls and gates that lock, and lots of separate little houses for the gardeners and people.

There is a *delicious* garden! I never saw such a garden – large and shady, full of box-bordered paths, and lined with long grape-covered arbors with seats under them.

There were greenhouses, too, but they are all broken now.

There was some legal trouble, I believe, something about the heirs and co-heirs; anyhow, the place has been empty for years.

That spoils my ghostliness, I am afraid, but I don't care – there is something strange about the house – I can feel it.

I even said so to John one moonlight evening, but he said what I felt was a *draught*, and shut the window.

I get unreasonably angry with John sometimes. I'm sure I never used to be so sensitive. I think it is due to this nervous condition.

But John says if I feel so, I shall neglect proper self-control; so I take pains to control myself – before him, at least, and that makes me very tired.

I don't like our room a bit. I wanted one downstairs that opened on the piazza and had roses all over the window, and such pretty old-fashioned chintz hangings! but John would not hear of it.

He said there was only one window and not room for two beds, and no near room for him if he took another.

He is very careful and loving, and hardly lets me stir without special direction.

I have a schedule prescription for each hour in the day; he takes all care from me, and so I feel basely ungrateful not to value it more.

He said we came here solely on my account, that I was

to have perfect rest and all the air I could get. 'Your exercise depends on your strength, my dear,' said he, 'and your food somewhat on your appetite; but air you can absorb all the time.' So we took the nursery at the top of the house.

It is a big, airy room, the whole floor nearly, with windows that look all ways, and air and sunshine galore. It was nursery first and then playroom and gymnasium, I should judge; for the windows are barred for little children, and there are rings and things in the walls.

The paint and paper look as if a boys' school had used it. It is stripped off – the paper – in great patches all around the head of my bed, about as far as I can reach, and in a great place on the other side of the room low down. I never saw a worse paper in my life.

One of those sprawling flamboyant patterns committing every artistic sin.

It is dull enough to confuse the eye in following, pronounced enough to constantly irritate and provoke study, and when you follow the lame uncertain curves for a little distance they suddenly commit suicide – plunge off at outrageous angles, destroy themselves in unheard of contradictions.

The color is repellant, almost revolting; a smouldering unclean yellow, strangely faded by the slow-turning sunlight.

It is a dull yet lurid orange in some places, a sickly sulphur tint in others.

No wonder the children hated it! I should hate it myself if I had to live in this room long.

There comes John, and I must put this away, – he hates to have me write a word.

We have been here two weeks, and I haven't felt like writing before, since that first day.

I am sitting by the window now, up in this atrocious nursery, and there is nothing to hinder my writing as much as I please, save lack of strength.

John is away all day, and even some nights when his cases are serious.

I am glad my case is not serious!

But these nervous troubles are dreadfully depressing.

John does not know how much I really suffer. He knows there is no *reason* to suffer, and that satisfies him.

Of course it is only nervousness. It does weigh on me so not to do my duty in any way!

I meant to be such a help to John, such a real rest and comfort, and here I am a comparative burden already!

Nobody would believe what an effort it is to do what little I am able, – to dress and entertain, and order things.

It is fortunate Mary is so good with the baby. Such a dear baby!

And yet I *cannot* be with him, it makes me so nervous.

I suppose John never was nervous in his life. He laughs at me so about this wall-paper!

At first he meant to repaper the room, but afterwards he said that I was letting it get the better of me, and that nothing was worse for a nervous patient than to give way to such fancies.

He said that after the wall-paper was changed it would be the heavy bedstead, and then the barred windows, and then that gate at the head of the stairs, and so on.

'You know the place is doing you good,' he said, 'and really, dear, I don't care to renovate the house just for a three months' rental.'

'Then do let us go downstairs,' I said, 'there are such pretty rooms there.'

Then he took me in his arms and called me a blessed little goose, and said he would go down to the cellar, if I wished, and have it whitewashed into the bargain.

But he is right enough about the beds and windows and things.

It is an airy and comfortable room as any one need wish, and, of course, I would not be so silly as to make him uncomfortable just for a whim.

I'm really getting quite fond of the big room, all but that horrid paper.

Out of one window I can see the garden, those mysterious deep-shaded arbors, the riotous old-fashioned flowers, and bushes and gnarly trees.

Out of another I get a lovely view of the bay and a little private wharf belonging to the estate. There is a beautiful shaded lane that runs down there from the house. I always fancy I see people walking in these numerous paths and arbors, but John has cautioned me not to give way to fancy in the least. He says that with my imaginative power and habit of story-making, a nervous weakness like mine is sure to lead to all manner of excited fancies, and that I ought to use my will and good sense to check the tendency. So I try.

I think sometimes that if I were only well enough to write a little it would relieve the press of ideas and rest me.

But I find I get pretty tired when I try.

It is so discouraging not to have any advice and companionship about my work. When I get really well, John says we will ask Cousin Henry and Julia down for a long visit; but he says he would as soon put fireworks in my pillow-case as to let me have those stimulating people about now.

I wish I could get well faster.

But I must not think about that. This paper looks to me as if it *knew* what a vicious influence it had!

There is a recurrent spot where the pattern lolls like a broken neck and two bulbous eyes stare at you upside down.

I get positively angry with the impertinence of it and the everlastingness. Up and down and sideways they crawl, and those absurd, unblinking eyes are everywhere. There is one place where two breadths didn't match, and the eyes go all up and down the line, one a little higher than the other.

I never saw so much expression in an inanimate thing before, and we all know how much expression they have! I used to lie awake as a child and get more entertainment and terror out of blank walls and plain furniture than most children could find in a toy-store.

I remember what a kindly wink the knobs of our big, old bureau used to have, and there was one chair that always seemed like a strong friend.

I used to feel that if any of the other things looked too fierce I could always hop into that chair and be safe.

The furniture in this room is no worse than inharmonious, however, for we had to bring it all from downstairs. I suppose when this was used as a playroom they had to take the nursery things out, and no wonder! I never saw such ravages as the children have made here.

The wall-paper, as I said before, is torn off in spots, and it sticketh closer than a brother – they must have had perseverance as well as hatred.

Then the floor is scratched and gouged and splintered, the plaster itself is dug out here and there, and this great heavy bed which is all we found in the room, looks as if it had been through the wars.

But I don't mind it a bit – only the paper.

There comes John's sister. Such a dear girl as she is, and so careful of me! I must not let her find me writing.

She is a perfect and enthusiastic housekeeper, and hopes for no better profession. I verily believe she thinks it is the writing which made me sick!

But I can write when she is out, and see her a long way off from these windows.

There is one that commands the road, a lovely shaded winding road, and one that just looks off over the country. A lovely country, too, full of great elms and velvet meadows.

This wallpaper has a kind of subpattern in a different shade, a particularly irritating one, for you can only see it in certain lights, and not clearly then.

But in the places where it isn't faded and where the sun is just so – I can see a strange, provoking, formless sort of figure, that seems to skulk about behind that silly and conspicuous front design.

There's sister on the stairs!

Well, the Fourth of July is over! The people are all gone and I am tired out. John thought it might do me good to see a little company, so we just had mother and Nellie and the children down for a week.

Of course I didn't do a thing. Jennie sees to everything now.

But it tired me all the same.

John says if I don't pick up faster he shall send me to Weir Mitchell in the fall.

But I don't want to go there at all. I had a friend who was in his hands once, and she says he is just like John and my brother, only more so!

Besides, it is such an undertaking to go so far.

I don't feel as if it was worth while to turn my hand over for anything, and I'm getting dreadfully fretful and querulous.

I cry at nothing, and cry most of the time.

Of course I don't when John is here, or anybody else, but when I am alone.

And I am alone a good deal just now. John is kept in town very often by serious cases, and Jennie is good and lets me alone when I want her to.

So I walk a little in the garden or down that lovely lane, sit on the porch under the roses, and lie down up here a good deal.

I'm getting really fond of the room in spite of the wall-paper. Perhaps *because* of the wall-paper.

It dwells in my mind so!

I lie here on this great immovable bed – it is nailed down, I believe – and follow that pattern about by the hour. It is as good as gymnastics, I assure you. I start, we'll say, at the bottom, down in the corner over there where it has not been touched, and I determine for the thousandth time that I *will* follow that pointless pattern to some sort of a conclusion.

I know a little of the principle of design, and I know this thing was not arranged on any laws of radiation, or alternation, or repetition, or symmetry, or anything else that I ever heard of.

It is repeated, of course, by the breadths, but not otherwise.

Looked at in one way each breadth stands alone, the bloated curves and flourishes – a kind of 'debased Romanesque' with *delirium tremens* – go waddling up and down in isolated columns of fatuity.

But, on the other hand, they connect diagonally, and the sprawling outlines run off in great slanting waves of optic horror, like a lot of wallowing seaweeds in full chase.

The whole thing goes horizontally, too, at least it seems so, and I exhaust myself in trying to distinguish the order of its going in that direction.

They have used a horizontal breadth for a frieze, and that adds wonderfully to the confusion.

There is one end of the room where it is almost intact, and there, when the crosslights fade and the low sun shines directly upon it, I can almost fancy radiation after all, – the interminable grotesques seem to form around a common centre and rush off in headlong plunges of equal distraction.

It makes me tired to follow it. I will take a nap I guess.

I don't know why I should write this.

I don't want to.

I don't feel able.

And I know John would think it absurd. But I *must* say what I feel and think in some way – it is such a relief!

But the effort is getting to be greater than the relief.

Half the time now I am awfully lazy, and lie down ever so much.

John says I mustn't lose my strength, and has me take cod liver oil and lots of tonics and things, to say nothing of ale and wine and rare meat.

Dear John! He loves me very dearly, and hates to have me sick. I tried to have a real earnest reasonable talk with him the other day, and tell him how I wish he would let me go and make a visit to Cousin Henry and Julia.

But he said I wasn't able to go, nor able to stand it after I got there; and I did not make out a very good case for myself, for I was crying before I had finished.

It is getting to be a great effort for me to think straight. Just this nervous weakness I suppose.

And dear John gathered me up in his arms, and just carried me upstairs and laid me on the bed, and sat by me and read to me till it tired my head.

He said I was his darling and his comfort and all he had, and that I must take care of myself for his sake, and keep well.

He says no one but myself can help me out of it, that I must use my will and self-control and not let any silly fancies run away with me.

There's one comfort, the baby is well and happy, and does not have to occupy this nursery with the horrid wallpaper.

If we had not used it, that blessed child would have!

What a fortunate escape! Why, I wouldn't have a child of mine, an impressionable little thing, live in such a room for worlds.

I never thought of it before, but it is lucky that John kept me here after all, I can stand it so much easier than a baby, you see.

Of course I never mention it to them any more – I am too wise, – but I keep watch of it all the same.

There are things in that paper that nobody knows but me, or ever will.

Behind that outside pattern the dim shapes get clearer every day.

It is always the same shape, only very numerous.

And it is like a woman stooping down and creeping about behind that pattern. I don't like it a bit. I wonder – I begin to think – I wish John would take me away from here!

It is so hard to talk with John about my case, because he is so wise, and because he loves me so.

But I tried it last night.

It was moonlight. The moon shines in all around just as the sun does.

I hate to see it sometimes, it creeps so slowly, and always comes in by one window or another.

John was asleep and I hated to waken him, so I kept still and watched the moonlight on that undulating wall-paper till I felt creepy.

The faint figure behind seemed to shake the pattern, just as if she wanted to get out.

I got up softly and went to feel and see if the paper *did* move, and when I came back John was awake.

'What is it, little girl?' he said. 'Don't go walking about like that – you'll get cold.'

I thought it was a good time to talk, so I told him that I really was not gaining here, and that I wished he would take me away.

'Why, darling!' said he, 'our lease will be up in three weeks, and I can't see how to leave before.

'The repairs are not done at home, and I cannot possibly leave town just now. Of course if you were in any danger, I could and would, but you really are better, dear, whether you can see it or not. I am a doctor, dear, and I know. You are gaining flesh and color, your appetite is better, I feel really much easier about you.'

'I don't weigh a bit more,' said I, 'nor as much; and my appetite may be better in the evening when you are here, but it is worse in the morning when you are away!'

'Bless her little heart!' said he with a big hug, 'she shall be as sick as she pleases! But now let's improve the shining hours by going to sleep, and talk about it in the morning!'

'And you won't go away?' I asked gloomily.

'Why, how can I, dear? It is only three weeks more and then we will take a nice little trip of a few days while

Jennie is getting the house ready. Really, dear, you are better!'

'Better in body perhaps –' I began, and stopped short, for he sat up straight and looked at me with such a stern, reproachful look that I could not say another word.

'My darling,' said he, 'I beg of you, for my sake and for our child's sake, as well as for your own, that you will never for one instant let that idea enter your mind! There is nothing so dangerous, so fascinating, to a temperament like yours. It is a false and foolish fancy. Can you not trust me as a physician when I tell you so?'

So of course I said no more on that score, and we went to sleep before long. He thought I was asleep first, but I wasn't, and lay there for hours trying to decide whether that front pattern and the back pattern really did move together or separately.

On a pattern like this, by daylight, there is a lack of sequence, a defiance of law, that is a constant irritant to a normal mind.

The color is hideous enough, and unreliable enough, and infuriating enough, but the pattern is torturing.

You think you have mastered it, but just as you get well underway in following, it turns a back-somersault and there you are. It slaps you in the face, knocks you down, and tramples upon you. It is like a bad dream.

The outside pattern is a florid arabesque, reminding

one of a fungus. If you can imagine a toadstool in joints, an interminable string of toadstools, budding and sprouting in endless convolutions – why, that is something like it.

That is, sometimes!

There is one marked peculiarity about this paper, a thing nobody seems to notice but myself, and that is that it changes as the light changes.

When the sun shoots in through the east window – I always watch for that first long, straight ray – it changes so quickly that I never can quite believe it.

That is why I watch it always.

By moonlight – the moon shines in all night when there is a moon – I wouldn't know it was the same paper.

At night in any kind of light, in twilight, candlelight, lamplight, and worst of all by moonlight, it becomes bars! The outside pattern I mean, and the woman behind it is as plain as can be.

I didn't realize for a long time what the thing was that showed behind, that dim sub-pattern, but now I am quite sure it is a woman.

By daylight she is subdued, quiet. I fancy it is the pattern that keeps her so still. It is so puzzling. It keeps me quiet by the hour.

I lie down ever so much now. John says it is good for me, and to sleep all I can.

Indeed he started the habit by making me lie down for an hour after each meal.

It is a very bad habit I am convinced, for you see I don't sleep.

And that cultivates deceit, for I don't tell them I'm awake – O no!

The fact is I am getting a little afraid of John.

He seems very queer sometimes, and even Jennie has an inexplicable look.

It strikes me occasionally, just as a scientific hypothesis, – that perhaps it is the paper!

I have watched John when he did not know I was looking, and come into the room suddenly on the most innocent excuses, and I've caught him several times *looking at the paper!* And Jennie too. I caught Jennie with her hand on it once.

She didn't know I was in the room, and when I asked her in a quiet, a very quiet voice, with the most restrained manner possible, what she was doing with the paper – she turned around as if she had been caught stealing, and looked quite angry – asked me why I should frighten her so!

Then she said that the paper stained everything it touched, that she had found yellow smooches on all my clothes and John's, and she wished we would be more careful!

Did not that sound innocent? But I know she was studying that pattern, and I am determined that nobody shall find it out but myself!

*

Life is very much more exciting now than it used to be. You see I have something more to expect, to look forward to, to watch. I really do eat better, and am more quiet than I was.

John is so pleased to see me improve! He laughed a little the other day, and said I seemed to be flourishing in spite of my wall-paper.

I turned it off with a laugh. I had no intention of telling him it was *because* of the wall-paper – he would make fun of me. He might even want to take me away.

I don't want to leave now until I have found it out. There is a week more, and I think that will be enough.

I'm feeling ever so much better! I don't sleep much at night, for it is so interesting to watch developments; but I sleep a good deal in the daytime.

In the daytime it is tiresome and perplexing.

There are always new shoots on the fungus, and new shades of yellow all over it. I cannot keep count of them, though I have tried conscientiously.

It is the strangest yellow, that wall-paper! It makes me think of all the yellow things I ever saw – not beautiful ones like buttercups, but old foul, bad yellow things.

But there is something else about that paper – the smell! I noticed it the moment we came into the room, but with so much air and sun it was not bad. Now we have had a week of fog and rain, and whether the windows are open or not, the smell is here.

It creeps all over the house.

I find it hovering in the dining-room, skulking in the parlor, hiding in the hall, lying in wait for me on the stairs.

It gets into my hair.

Even when I go to ride, if I turn my head suddenly and surprise it – there is that smell!

Such a peculiar odor, too! I have spent hours in trying to analyze it, to find what it smelled like.

It is not bad – at first, and very gentle, but quite the subtlest, most enduring odor I ever met.

In this damp weather it is awful, I wake up in the night and find it hanging over me.

It used to disturb me at first. I thought seriously of burning the house – to reach the smell.

But now I am used to it. The only thing I can think of that it is like is the *color* of the paper! A yellow smell.

There is a very funny mark on this wall, low down, near the mopboard. A streak that runs round the room. It goes behind every piece of furniture, except the bed, a long, straight, even *smooch*, as if it had been rubbed over and over.

I wonder how it was done and who did it, and what they did it for. Round and round and round – round and round and round – it makes me dizzy!

I really have discovered something at last.

Through watching so much at night, when it changes so, I have finally found out.

The front pattern *does* move – and no wonder! The woman behind shakes it!

Sometimes I think there are a great many women behind, and sometimes only one, and she crawls around fast, and her crawling shakes it all over.

Then in the very bright spots she keeps still, and in the very shady spots she just takes hold of the bars and shakes them hard.

And she is all the time trying to climb through. But nobody could climb through that pattern – it strangles so; I think that is why it has so many heads.

They get through, and then the pattern strangles them off and turns them upside down, and makes their eyes white!

If those heads were covered or taken off it would not be half so bad.

I think that woman gets out in the daytime!

And I'll tell you why – privately – I've seen her!

I can see her out of every one of my windows!

It is the same woman, I know, for she is always creeping, and most women do not creep by daylight.

I see her in that long shaded lane, creeping up and down. I see her in those dark grape arbors, creeping all around the garden.

I see her on that long road under the trees, creeping along, and when a carriage comes she hides under the blackberry vines.

I don't blame her a bit. It must be very humiliating to be caught creeping by daylight!

I always lock the door when I creep by daylight. I can't do it at night, for I know John would suspect something at once.

And John is so queer now, that I don't want to irritate him. I wish he would take another room! Besides, I don't want anybody to get that woman out at night but myself.

I often wonder if I could see her out of all the windows at once.

But, turn as fast as I can, I can only see out of one at one time.

And though I always see her, she *may* be able to creep faster than I can turn!

I have watched her sometimes away off in the open country, creeping as fast as a cloud shadow in a high wind.

If only that top pattern could be gotten off from the under one! I mean to try it, little by little.

I have found out another funny thing, but I shan't tell it this time! It does not do to trust people too much.

There are only two more days to get this paper off, and I believe John is beginning to notice. I don't like the look in his eyes.

And I heard him ask Jennie a lot of professional questions about me. She had a very good report to give.

She said I slept a good deal in the daytime.

John knows I don't sleep very well at night, for all I'm so quiet!

He asked me all sorts of questions, too, and pretended to be very loving and kind.

As if I couldn't see through him!

Still, I don't wonder he acts so, sleeping under this paper for three months.

It only interests me, but I feel sure John and Jennie are secretly affected by it.

Hurrah! This is the last day, but it is enough. John is to stay in town over night, and won't be out until this evening.

Jennie wanted to sleep with me – the sly thing! but I told her I should undoubtedly rest better for a night all alone.

That was clever, for really I wasn't alone a bit! As soon as it was moonlight and that poor thing began to crawl and shake the pattern, I got up and ran to help her.

I pulled and she shook, I shook and she pulled, and before morning we had peeled off yards of that paper.

A strip about as high as my head and half around the room.

And then when the sun came and that awful pattern began to laugh at me, I declared I would finish it to-day!

We go away to-morrow, and they are moving all my furniture down again to leave things as they were before.

Jennie looked at the wall in amazement, but I told her merrily that I did it out of pure spite at the vicious thing.

She laughed and said she wouldn't mind doing it herself, but I must not get tired.

How she betrayed herself that time!

But I am here, and no person touches this paper but me, – not *alive!*

She tried to get me out of the room – it was too patent! But I said it was so quiet and empty and clean now that I believed I would lie down again and sleep all I could; and not to wake me even for dinner – I would call when I woke.

So now she is gone, and the servants are gone, and the things are gone, and there is nothing left but that great bedstead nailed down, with the canvas mattress we found on it.

We shall sleep downstairs to-night, and take the boat home tomorrow.

I quite enjoy the room, now it is bare again.

How those children did tear about here!

This bedstead is fairly gnawed!

But I must get to work.

I have locked the door and thrown the key down into the front path.

I don't want to go out, and I don't want to have anybody come in, till John comes.

I want to astonish him.

I've got a rope up here that even Jennie did not find. If that woman does get out, and tries to get away, I can tie her!

But I forgot I could not reach far without anything to stand on!

This bed will *not* move!

I tried to lift and push it until I was lame, and then I got so angry I bit off a little piece at one corner – but it hurt my teeth.

Then I peeled off all the paper I could reach standing on the floor. It sticks horribly and the pattern just enjoys it! All those strangled heads and bulbous eyes and waddling fungus growths just shriek with derision!

I am getting angry enough to do something desperate. To jump out of the window would be admirable exercise, but the bars are too strong even to try.

Besides I wouldn't do it. Of course not. I know well enough that a step like that is improper and might be misconstrued.

I don't like to *look* out of the windows even – there are so many of those creeping women, and they creep so fast.

I wonder if they all come out of that wall-paper as I did?

But I am securely fastened now by my well-hidden rope – you don't get *me* out in the road there!

I suppose I shall have to get back behind the pattern when it comes night, and that is hard!

It is so pleasant to be out in this great room and creep around as I please!

I don't want to go outside. I won't, even if Jennie asks me to.

For outside you have to creep on the ground, and everything is green instead of yellow.

But here I can creep smoothly on the floor, and my shoulder just fits in that long smooch around the wall, so I cannot lose my way.

Why there's John at the door!

It is no use, young man, you can't open it!

How he does call and pound!

Now he's crying for an axe.

It would be a shame to break down that beautiful door!

'John dear!' said I in the gentlest voice, 'the key is down by the front steps, under a plantain leaf!'

That silenced him for a few moments.

Then he said – very quietly indeed, 'Open the door, my darling!'

'I can't,' said I. 'The key is down by the front door under a plantain leaf!'

And then I said it again, several times, very gently and slowly, and said it so often that he had to go and see, and he got it of course, and came in. He stopped short by the door.

'What is the matter?' he cried. 'For God's sake, what are you doing!'

I kept on creeping just the same, but I looked at him over my shoulder.

'I've got out at last,' said I, 'in spite of you and Jane! And I've pulled off most of the paper, so you can't put me back!'

Now why should that man have fainted? But he did, and right across my path by the wall, so that I had to creep over him every time!

The Rocking-Chair

A waving spot of sunshine, a signal light that caught the eye at once in a waste of commonplace houses, and all the dreary dimness of a narrow city street.

Across some low roof that made a gap in the wall of masonry, shot a level, brilliant beam of the just-setting sun, touching the golden head of a girl in an open window.

She sat in a high-backed rocking-chair with brass mountings that glittered as it swung, rocking slowly back and forth, never lifting her head, but fairly lighting up the street with the glory of her sunlit hair.

We two stopped and stared, and, so staring, caught sight of a small sign in a lower window – 'Furnished Lodgings.' With a common impulse we crossed the street and knocked at the dingy front door.

Slow, even footsteps approached from within, and a soft girlish laugh ceased suddenly as the door opened, showing us an old woman, with a dull, expressionless face and faded eyes.

Yes, she had rooms to let. Yes, we could see them. No, there was no service. No, there were no meals. So murmuring monotonously, she led the way up-stairs. It was an ordinary house enough, on a poor sort of street, a house in no way remarkable or unlike its fellows.

She showed us two rooms, connected, neither better nor worse than most of their class, rooms without a striking feature about them, unless it was the great brass-bound chair we found still rocking gently by the window.

But the gold-haired girl was nowhere to be seen.

I fancied I heard the light rustle of girlish robes in the inner chamber – a breath of that low laugh – but the door leading to this apartment was locked, and when I asked the woman if we could see the other rooms she said she had no other rooms to let.

A few words aside with Hal, and we decided to take these two, and move in at once. There was no reason we should not. We were looking for lodgings when that swinging sunbeam caught our eyes, and the accommodations were fully as good as we could pay for. So we closed our bargain on the spot, returned to our deserted boarding-house for a few belongings, and were settled anew that night.

Hal and I were young newspaper men, 'penny-a-liners,' part of that struggling crowd of aspirants who are to literature what squires and pages were to knighthood in olden days. We were winning our spurs. So far it was slow work, unpleasant and ill-paid – so was squireship and pagehood, I am sure; menial service and laborious polishing of armor; long running afoot while the master rode. But the squire could at least honor his lord and leader, while we, alas! had small honor for those above us in our profession, with but too good reason. We, of course, should do far nobler things when these same spurs were won!

Now it may have been mere literary instinct – the grasping at 'material' of the pot-boiling writers of the day, and it may have been another kind of instinct – the unacknowledged attraction of the fair unknown; but, whatever the reason, the place had drawn us both, and here we were.

Unbroken friendship begun in babyhood held us two together, all the more closely because Hal was a merry, prosaic, clear-headed fellow, and I sensitive and romantic.

The fearless frankness of family life we shared, but held the right to unapproachable reserves, and so kept love unstrained.

We examined our new quarters with interest. The front room, Hal's, was rather big and bare. The back room, mine, rather small and bare.

He preferred that room, I am convinced, because of the window and the chair. I preferred the other, because of the locked door. We neither of us mentioned these prejudices.

'Are you sure you would not rather have this room?' asked Hal, conscious, perhaps, of an ulterior motive in his choice.

'No, indeed,' said I, with a similar reservation; 'you

only have the street and I have a real "view" from my window. The only thing I begrudge you is the chair!'

'You may come and rock therein at any hour of the day or night,' said he magnanimously. 'It is tremendously comfortable, for all its black looks.'

It was a comfortable chair, a very comfortable chair, and we both used it a great deal. A very high-backed chair, curving a little forward at the top, with heavy square corners. These corners, the ends of the rockers, the great sharp knobs that tipped the arms, and every other point and angle were mounted in brass.

'Might be used for a battering-ram!' said Hal.

He sat smoking in it, rocking slowly and complacently by the window, while I lounged on the foot of the bed, and watched a pale young moon sink slowly over the western housetops.

It went out of sight at last, and the room grew darker and darker till I could only see Hal's handsome head and the curving chair-back move slowly to and fro against the dim sky.

'What brought us here so suddenly, Maurice?' he asked, out of the dark.

'Three reasons,' I answered. 'Our need of lodgings, the suitability of these, and a beautiful head.'

'Correct,' said he. 'Anything else?'

'Nothing you would admit the existence of, my sternly logical friend. But I am conscious of a certain compulsion, or at least attraction, in the case, which does not seem wholly accounted for, even by golden hair.'

'For once I will agree with you,' said Hal. 'I feel the same way myself, and I am not impressionable.'

We were silent for a little. I may have closed my eyes, – it may have been longer than I thought, but it did not seem another moment when something brushed softly against my arm, and Hal in his great chair was rocking beside me.

'Excuse me,' said he, seeing me start. 'This chair evidently "walks," I've seen 'em before.'

So had I, on carpets, but there was no carpet here, and I thought I was awake.

He pulled the heavy thing back to the window again, and we went to bed.

Our door was open, and we could talk back and forth, but presently I dropped off and slept heavily until morning. But I must have dreamed most vividly, for he accused me of rocking in his chair half the night, said he could see my outline clearly against the starlight.

'No,' said I, 'you dreamed it. You've got that rocking-chair on the brain.'

'Dream it is, then,' he answered cheerily. 'Better a nightmare than a contradiction; a vampire than a quarrel! Come on, let's go to breakfast!'

We wondered greatly as the days went by that we saw nothing of our golden-haired charmer. But we wondered in silence, and neither mentioned it to the other.

31

Sometimes I heard her light movements in the room next mine, or the soft laugh somewhere in the house; but the mother's slow, even steps were more frequent, and even she was not often visible.

All either of us saw of the girl, to my knowledge, was from the street, for she still availed herself of our chair by the window. This we disapproved of, on principle, the more so as we left the doors locked, and her presence proved the possession of another key. No; there was the door in my room! But I did not mention the idea. Under the circumstances, however, we made no complaint, and used to rush stealthily and swiftly up-stairs, hoping to surprise her. But we never succeeded. Only the chair was often found still rocking, and sometimes I fancied a faint sweet odor lingering about, an odor strangely saddening and suggestive. But one day when I thought Hal was there I rushed in unceremoniously and caught her. It was but a glimpse – a swift, light, noiseless sweep – she vanished into my own room. Following her with apologies for such a sudden entrance, I was too late. The envious door was locked again.

Our landlady's fair daughter was evidently shy enough when brought to bay, but strangely willing to take liberties in our absence.

Still, I had seen her, and for that sight would have forgiven much. Hers was a strange beauty, infinitely attractive yet infinitely perplexing. I marveled in secret, and longed with painful eagerness for another meeting;

but I said nothing to Hal of my surprising her – it did not seem fair to the girl! She might have some good reason for going there; perhaps I could meet her again.

So I took to coming home early, on one excuse or another, and inventing all manner of errands to get to the room when Hal was not in.

But it was not until after numberless surprises on that point, finding him there when I supposed him downtown, and noticing something a little forced in his needless explanations, that I began to wonder if he might not be on the same quest.

Soon I was sure of it. I reached the corner of the street one evening just at sunset, and – yes, there was the rhythmic swing of that bright head in the dark frame of the open window. There also was Hal in the street below. She looked out, she smiled. He let himself in and went up-stairs.

I quickened my pace. I was in time to see the movement stop, the fair head turn, and Hal standing beyond her in the shadow.

I passed the door, passed the street, walked an hour – two hours – got a late supper somewhere, and came back about bedtime with a sharp and bitter feeling in my heart that I strove in vain to reason down. Why he had not as good a right to meet her as I it were hard to say, and yet I was strangely angry with him.

When I returned the lamplight shone behind the white curtain, and the shadow of the great chair stood motionless against it. Another shadow crossed – Hal – smoking. I went up.

He greeted me effusively and asked why I was so late. Where I got supper. Was unnaturally cheerful. There was a sudden dreadful sense of concealment between us. But he told nothing and I asked nothing, and we went silently to bed.

I blamed him for saying no word about our fair mystery, and yet I had said none concerning my own meeting. I racked my brain with questions as to how much he had really seen of her; if she had talked to him; what she had told him; how long she had stayed.

I tossed all night and Hal was sleepless too, for I heard him rocking for hours, by the window, by the bed, close to my door. I never knew a rocking-chair to 'walk' as that one did.

Towards morning the steady creak and swing was too much for my nerves or temper.

'For goodness' sake, Hal, do stop that and go to bed!'

'What?' came a sleepy voice.

'Don't fool!' said I, 'I haven't slept a wink to-night for your everlasting rocking. Now do leave off and go to bed.'

'Go to bed! I've been in bed all night and I wish you had! Can't you use the chair without blaming me for it?'

And all the time I *heard* him rock, rock, rock, over by the hall door!

I rose stealthily and entered the room, meaning to surprise the ill-timed joker and convict him in the act.

Both rooms were full of the dim phosphorescence of reflected moonlight; I knew them even in the dark; and yet I stumbled just inside the door, and fell heavily.

Hal was out of bed in a moment and had struck a light. 'Are you hurt, my dear boy?'

I was hurt, and solely by his fault, for the chair was not where I supposed, but close to my bedroom door, where he must have left it to leap into bed when he heard me coming. So it was in no amiable humor that I refused his offers of assistance and limped back to my own sleepless pillow. I had struck my ankle on one of those brass-tipped rockers, and it pained me severely. I never saw a chair so made to hurt as that one. It was so large and heavy and ill-balanced, and every joint and corner so shod with brass. Hal and I had punished ourselves enough on it before, especially in the dark when we forgot where the thing was standing, but never so severely as this. It was not like Hal to play such tricks, and both heart and ankle ached as I crept into bed again to toss and doze and dream and fitfully start till morning.

Hal was kindness itself, but he would insist that he had been asleep and I rocking all night, till I grew actually angry with him.

'That's carrying a joke too far,' I said at last. 'I don't mind a joke, even when it hurts, but there are limits.'

'Yes, there are!' said he, significantly, and we dropped the subject.

Several days passed. Hal had repeated meetings with

the gold-haired damsel; this I saw from the street; but save for these bitter glimpses I waited vainly.

It was hard to bear, harder almost than the growing estrangement between Hal and me, and that cut deeply. I think that at last either one of us would have been glad to go away by himself, but neither was willing to leave the other to the room, the chair, the beautiful unknown.

Coming home one morning unexpectedly, I found the dull-faced landlady arranging the rooms, and quite laid myself out to make an impression upon her, to no purpose.

'That is a fine old chair you have there,' said I, as she stood mechanically polishing the brass corners with her apron.

She looked at the darkly glittering thing with almost a flash of pride.

'Yes,' said she, 'a fine chair!'

'Is it old?' I pursued.

'Very old,' she answered briefly.

'But I thought rocking-chairs were a modern American invention?' said I.

She looked at me apathetically.

'It is Spanish,' she said, 'Spanish oak, Spanish leather, Spanish brass, Spanish —.' I did not catch the last word, and she left the room without another.

It was a strange ill-balanced thing, that chair, though so easy and comfortable to sit in. The rockers were long and sharp behind, always lying in wait for the unwary, but cut short in front: and the back was so high and so heavy on top, that what with its weight and the shortness of the front rockers, it tipped forward with an ease and a violence equally astonishing.

This I knew from experience, as it had plunged over upon me during some of our frequent encounters. Hal also was a sufferer, but in spite of our manifold bruises, neither of us would have had the chair removed, for did not she sit in it, evening after evening, and rock there in the golden light of the setting sun.

So, evening after evening, we two fled from our work as early as possible, and hurried home alone, by separate ways, to the dingy street and the glorified window.

I could not endure forever. When Hal came home first, I, lingering in the street below, could see through our window that lovely head and his in close proximity. When I came first, it was to catch perhaps a quick glance from above – a bewildering smile – no more. She was always gone when I reached the room, and the inner door of my chamber irrevocably locked.

At times I even caught the click of the latch, heard the flutter of loose robes on the other side; and sometimes this daily disappointment, this constant agony of hope deferred, would bring me to my knees by that door begging her to open to me, crying to her in every term of passionate endearment and persuasion that tortured heart of man could think to use.

Hal had neither word nor look for me now, save those

of studied politeness and cold indifference, and how could I behave otherwise to him, so proven to my face a liar?

I saw him from the street one night, in the broad level sunlight, sitting in that chair, with the beautiful head on his shoulder. It was more than I could bear. If he had won, and won so utterly, I would ask but to speak to her once, and say farewell to both forever. So I heavily climbed the stairs, knocked loudly, and entered at Hal's 'Come in!' only to find him sitting there alone, smoking – yes, smoking in the chair which but a moment since had held her too!

He had but just lit the cigar, a paltry device to blind my eyes.

'Look here, Hal,' said I, 'I can't stand this any longer. May I ask you one thing? Let me see her once, just once, that I may say good-bye, and then neither of you need see me again!'

Hal rose to his feet and looked me straight in the eye. Then he threw that whole cigar out of the window, and walked to within two feet of me.

'Are you crazy,' he said. '*I* ask her! *I*! I have never had speech of her in my life! And *you* –' He stopped and turned away.

'And I what?' I would have it out now whatever came.

'And you have seen her day after day – talked with her – I need not repeat all that my eyes have seen!'

'You need not, indeed,' said I. 'It would tax even your

invention. I have never seen her in this room but once, and then but for a fleeting glimpse – no word. From the street I have seen her often – with you!'

He turned very white and walked from me to the window, then turned again.

'I have never seen her in this room for even such a moment as you own to. From the street I have seen her often – *with you!*'

We looked at each other.

'Do you mean to say,' I inquired slowly, 'that I did not see you just now sitting in that chair, by that window, with her in your arms?'

'Stop!' he cried, throwing out his hand with a fierce gesture. It struck sharply on the corner of the chair-back. He wiped the blood mechanically from the three-cornered cut, looking fixedly at me.

'I saw you,' said I.

'You did not!' said he.

I turned slowly on my heel and went into my room. I could not bear to tell that man, my more than brother, that he lied.

I sat down on my bed with my head on my hands, and presently I heard Hal's door open and shut, his step on the stair, the front door slam behind him. He had gone, I knew not where, and if he went to his death and a word of mine would have stopped him, I would not have said it. I do not know how long I sat there, in the company of hopeless love and jealousy and hate.

Suddenly, out of the silence of the empty room, came the steady swing and creak of the great chair. Perhaps – it must be! I sprang to my feet and noiselessly opened the door. There she sat by the window, looking out, and – yes – she threw a kiss to some one below. Ah, how beautiful she was! How beautiful! I made a step toward her. I held out my hands, I uttered I know not what – when all at once came Hal's quick step upon the stairs.

She heard it, too, and, giving me one look, one subtle, mysterious, triumphant look, slipped past me and into my room just as Hal burst in. He saw her go. He came straight to me and I thought he would have struck me down where I stood.

'Out of my way,' he cried. 'I will speak to her. Is it not enough to see?' – he motioned toward the window with his wounded hand – 'Let me pass!'

'She is not there,' I answered. 'She has gone through into the other room.'

A light laugh sounded close by us, a faint, soft, silver laugh, almost at my elbow.

He flung me from his path, threw open the door, and entered. The room was empty.

'Where have you hidden her?' he demanded. I coldly pointed to the other door.

'So her room opens into yours, does it?' he muttered with a bitter smile. 'No wonder you preferred the "view"! Perhaps I can open it too?' And he laid his hand upon the latch.

I smiled then, for bitter experience had taught me that it was always locked, locked to all my prayers and entreaties. Let him kneel there as I had! But it opened under his hand! I sprang to his side, and we looked into – a closet, two by four, as bare and shallow as an empty coffin!

He turned to me, as white with rage as I was with terror. I was not thinking of him.

'What have you done with her?' he cried. And then contemptuously – 'That I should stop to question a liar!'

I paid no heed to him, but walked back into the other room, where the great chair rocked by the window.

He followed me, furious with disappointment, and laid his hand upon the swaying back, his strong fingers closing on it till the nails were white.

'Will you leave this place?' said he.

'No,' said I.

'I will live no longer with a liar and a traitor,' said he.

'Then you will have to kill yourself,' said I.

With a muttered oath he sprang upon me, but caught his foot in the long rocker, and fell heavily.

So wild a wave of hate rose in my heart that I could have trampled upon him where he lay – killed him like a dog – but with a mighty effort I turned from him and left the room.

When I returned it was broad day. Early and still, not sunrise yet, but full of hard, clear light on roof and wall and roadway. I stopped on the lower floor to find the landlady and announce my immediate departure. Door after door I knocked at, tried and opened; room after room I entered and searched thoroughly; in all that house, from cellar to garret, was no furnished room but ours, no sign of human occupancy. Dust, dust, and cobwebs everywhere. Nothing else.

With a strange sinking of the heart I came back to our own door.

Surely I heard the landlady's slow, even step inside, and that soft, low laugh. I rushed in.

The room was empty of all life; both rooms utterly empty.

Yes, of all life; for, with the love of a lifetime surging in my heart, I sprang to where Hal lay beneath the window, and found him dead.

Dead, and most horribly dead. Three heavy marks – blows – three deep, three-cornered gashes – I started to my feet – even the chair had gone!

Again the whispered laugh. Out of that house of terror I fled desperately.

From the street I cast one shuddering glance at the fateful window.

The risen sun was gilding all the housetops, and its level rays, striking the high panes on the building opposite, shone back in a calm glory on the great chair by the window, the sweet face, down-dropped eyes, and swaying golden head.

Old Water

The lake lay glassy in level golden light. Where the long shadows of the wooded bank spread across it was dark, fathomless. Where the little cliff rose on the eastern shore its bright reflection went down endlessly.

Slowly across the open gold came a still canoe, sent swiftly and smoothly on by well-accustomed arms.

'How strong! How splendid! Ah! she is like a Valkyr!' said the poet; and Mrs Osgood looked up at the dark bulk with appreciative eyes.

'You don't know how it delights me to have you speak like that!' she said softly. 'I feel those things myself, but have not the gift of words. And Ellen is so practical.'

'She could not be your daughter and not have a poetic soul,' he answered, smiling gravely.

'I'm sure I hope so. But I have never felt sure! When she was little I read to her from the poets, always; but she did not care for them – unless it was what she called "story poetry." And as soon as she had any choice of her own she took to science.'

'The poetry is there,' he said, his eyes on the smooth brown arms, now more near. 'That poise! That motion!

It is the very soul of poetry – and the body! Her body is a poem!'

Mrs Osgood watched the accurate landing, the strong pull that brought the canoe over the roller and up into the little boathouse. 'Ellen is so practical!' she murmured. 'She will not even admit her own beauty.'

'She is unawakened,' breathed the poet – 'Unawakened!' And his big eyes glimmered as with a stir of hope.

'It's very brave of her, too,' the mother went on. 'She does not really love the water, and just makes herself go out on it. I think in her heart she's afraid – but will not admit it. O Ellen! Come here dear. This is Mr Pendexter – the Poet.'

Ellen gave her cool brown hand; a little wet even, as she had casually washed them at the water's edge; but he pressed it warmly, and uttered his admiration of her skill with the canoe.

'O that's nothing,' said the girl. 'Canoeing's dead easy.'

'Will you teach it to me?' he asked. 'I will be a most docile pupil.'

She looked up and down his large frame with a somewhat questioning eye. It was big enough surely, and those great limbs must mean strength; but he lacked something of the balance and assured quickness which speaks of training.

'Can't you paddle?' she said.

'Forgive my ignorance – but I have never been in one of those graceful slim crafts. I shall be so glad to try.'

'Mr Pendexter has been more in Europe than America,' her mother put in hastily, 'and you must not imagine, my dear, that all men care for these things. I'm sure that if you are interested, my daughter will be very glad to teach you, Mr Pendexter.'

'Certainly,' said Ellen. 'I'll teach him in two tries. Want to start tomorrow morning? I'm usually out pretty early.'

'I shall be delighted,' he said. 'We will greet Aurora together.'

'The Dawn, dear,' suggested her mother with an apologetic smile.

'O yes,' the girl agreed. 'I recognize Aurora, mama. Is dinner ready?'

'It will be when you are dressed,' said her mother. 'Put on your blue frock, dear – the light one.'

'All right,' said Ellen, and ran lightly up the path.

'Beautiful! Beautiful!' he murmured, his eyes following her flying figure. 'Ah, madam! What it must be to you to have such a daughter! To see your own youth – but a moment passed – repeated before your eyes!' And he bent an admiring glance on the outlines of his hostess.

Mrs Osgood appeared at dinner in a somewhat classic gown, her fine hair banded with barbaric gold; and looked with satisfaction at her daughter, who shone like a juvenile Juno in her misty blue. Ellen had her mother's beauty and her father's strength. Her frame was large, her muscles had power under their flowing grace of line. She

45

carried herself like a queen, but wore the cheerful uncon-
scious air of a healthy schoolgirl, which she was.

Her appetite was so hearty that her mother almost
feared it would pain the poet, but she soon observed that
he too showed full appreciation of her chef's creations.
Ellen too observed him, noting with frank disapproval
that he ate freely of sweets and creams, and seemed to
enjoy the coffee and liqueurs exceedingly.

'Ellen never takes coffee,' Mrs Osgood explained, as
they sat in the luxurious drawing room, 'she has some
notion about training I believe.'

'Mother! I am training!' the girl protested. 'Not
officially – there's no race on; but I like to keep in good
condition. I'm stroke at college, Mr Pindexter.'

'*Pen*dexter, dear,' her mother whispered.

The big man took his second demitasse, and sat near
the girl.

'I can't tell you how much I admire it,' he said, leaning
forward. 'You are like Nausicaa – like Atalanta – like the
women of my dreams!'

She was not displeased with his open admiration – even
athletic girls are not above enjoying praise – but she took
it awkwardly.

'I don't believe in dreams,' she said.

'No,' he agreed, 'No – one must not. And yet – have
you never had a dream that haunts you – a dream that
comes again?'

'I've had bad dreams,' she admitted, 'horrid ones; but not the same dream twice.'

'What do you dream of when your dreams are terrible?'

'Beasts,' she answered promptly. 'Big beasts that jump at me! And I run and run – ugh!'

Mrs Osgood sipped her coffee and watched them. There was no young poet more promising than this. He represented all that her own girlhood had longed for – all that the highly prosperous mill-owner she married had utterly failed to give. If her daughter could have what she had missed!

'They say those dreams come from our remote past,' she suggested. 'Do you believe that, Mr Pendexter?'

'Yes,' he agreed, 'from our racial infancy. From those long buried years of fear and pain.'

'And when we have that queer feeling of *having been there before* – isn't that the same thing?'

'We do not know,' said he. 'Some say it is from a moment's delay in action of one-half of the brain. I cannot tell. To me it is more mysterious, more interesting, to think that when one has that wonderful sudden sense of previous acquaintance it means vague memories of a former life.' And he looked at Ellen as if she had figured largely in his previous existence. 'Have you ever had that feeling, Miss Osgood?'

The girl laughed rather shamefacedly. 'I've had it about one thing,' she said. 'That's why I'm afraid of water.'

'Afraid of water! You! A water goddess!'

'O, I don't encourage it, of course. But it's the only thing I ever was nervous about. I've had it from childhood – that horrid feeling!'

She shivered a little, and asked if he wouldn't like some music.

'Ah! You make music too?'

She laughed gaily. 'Only with the pianola – or the other machine. Shall I start it?'

'A moment,' he said. 'In a moment. But tell me, will you not, of this dream of something terrible? I am so deeply interested.'

'Why, it isn't much,' she said. 'I don't dream it, really – it comes when I'm awake. Only two or three times – once when I was about ten or eleven, and twice since. It's water – black, still, smooth water – way down below me. And I can't get away from it. I want to – and then something grabs me – ugh!'

She got up decidedly and went to the music stand. 'If that's a relic of my past I must have been prematurely cut off by an enraged ape! Anyhow, I don't like water – unless it's wild ocean. What shall I play?'

He meant to rise next morning with the daylight, but failed to awaken; and when he did look out he saw the canoe shooting lightly home in time for breakfast.

She laughed at him for his laziness, but promised a lesson later, and was pleased to find that he could play tennis. He looked well in his white flannels, in fact his appearance was more admirable than his playing, and the girl beat him till he grew almost angry.

Mrs Osgood watched delightedly on occasions where watching was agreeable, and on other occasions she took herself off with various excuses, and left them much together.

He expressed to her privately a question as to whether he was not too heavy for the canoe, but she reassured him.

'O, no, indeed, Mr Pendexter; it's a specially wide canoe, and has air chambers in it – it can't sink.' Her father had made it for her. 'He's a heavy man himself, and loves canoeing.'

So the stalwart poet was directed to step softly into the middle, and given the bow paddle.

It grieved him much that he could not see his fair instructress, and he proposed that they change places.

'No, indeed!' she said. 'Trust you with the other paddle? – Not yet!'

Could he not at least face her, he suggested. At which she laughed wickedly, and told him he'd better learn to paddle forward before he tried to do it backward.

'If you want to look at me you might get another canoe and try to follow,' she added, smiling; whereat he declared her would obey orders absolutely.

He sat all across the little rattan bow seat, and rolled up his sleeves as she did. She gave him the paddle, showed him how to hold it, and grinned silently as his mighty strokes swung them to right or left, for all her vigorous steering.

'Not so hard!' she said. 'You are stronger than I, and your stroke is so far out you swing me around.'

With a little patience he mastered the art sufficiently to wield a fairly serviceable bow paddle, but she would not trust him with the stern; and not all the beauties of the quiet lake consoled him for losing sight of her. Still, he reflected, she could see him. Perhaps that was why she kept him there in front! – and he sat straighter at the thought.

She did rather enjoy the well proportioned bulk of him, but she had small respect for his lack of dexterity, and felt a real dislike for the heavy fell of black hair on his arms and hands.

He tired of canoeing. One cannot direct speaking glances over one's shoulder, nor tender words; not with good effect, that is. At tennis he found her so steadily victor that he tired of that too. Golf she did not care for; horses he was unfamiliar with; and when she ran the car her hands and eyes and whole attention were on the machine. So he begged for walking.

'You must having charming walks in these woods,' he said. 'I own inferiority in many ways – but I can walk!'

'All right,' she cheerily agreed, and tramped about the country with him, brisk and tireless.

Her mother watched breathlessly. She wholly admired

this ox-eyed man with the velvet voice, the mouth so red under his soft mustache. She thought his poetry noble and musical beyond measure. Ellen thought it was 'no mortal use.'

'What on earth does he want to make over those old legends for, anyway!' she said, when her mother tried to win her to some appreciation. 'Isn't there enough to write about today without going back to people who never existed anyhow – nothing but characters out of other people's stories?'

'They are parts of the world's poetic material, my dear; folk-lore, race-myths. They are among our universal images.'

'Well, I don't like poetry about universal images, that's all. It's like mummies – sort of warmed over and dressed up!'

'I am so sorry!' said her mother, with some irritation. 'Here we are honored with a visit from one of our very greatest poets – perhaps the greatest; and my own child hasn't sense enough to appreciate his beautiful work. You are so like your father!'

'Well, I can't help it,' said Ellen. 'I don't like those foolish old stories about people who never did anything useful, and hadn't an idea in their heads except being in love and killing somebody! They had no sense, and no courage, and no decency!'

Her mother tried to win her to some admission of merit in his other work.

'It's no use, mama! You may have your poet, and get all the esthetic satisfaction you can out of it. And I'll be polite to him, of course. But I don't like his stuff.'

'Not his "Lyrics of the Day," dear? And "The Woods"?'

'No, mumsy, not even those. I don't believe he ever saw a sunrise – unless he got up on purpose and set himself before it like a camera! And woods! Why he don't know one tree from another!'

Her mother almost despaired of her; but the poet was not discouraged.

'Ah! Mrs Osgood! Since you honor me with your confidence I can but thank you and try my fate. It is so beautiful, this budding soul – not opened yet! So close – so almost hard! But when its rosy petals do unfold –'

He did not, however, give his confidence to Mrs Osgood beyond this gentle poetic outside view of a sort of floricultural intent. He told her nothing of the storm of passion which was growing within him; a passion of such seething intensity as would have alarmed that gentle soul exceedingly and make her doubt, perhaps, the wisdom of her selection.

She remained in a state of eager but restrained emotion; saying little to Ellen lest she alarm her, but hoping that the girl would find happiness with this great soul.

The great soul, meanwhile, pursued his way, using every art he knew – and his experience was not narrow – to reach the heart of the brown and ruddy nymph beside him.

She was ignorant and young. Too whole-souled in her

indifference to really appreciate the stress he labored under; much less to sympathize. On the contrary she took a mischievous delight in teasing him, doing harm without knowing it, like a playful child. She teased him about his tennis playing, about his paddling, about his driving; allowed that perhaps he might play golf well, but she didn't care for golf herself – it was too slow; mocked even his walking expeditions.

'He don't want to walk!' she said gaily to her mother one night at dinner. 'He just wants to go somewhere and arrange himself gracefully under a tree and read to me about Eloise, or Araminta or somebody; all slim and white and wavy and golden-haired; and how they killed themselves for love!'

She laughed frankly at him, and he laughed with her; but his heart was hot and dark within him. The longer he pursued and failed the fiercer was his desire for her. Already he had loved longer than was usual to him. Never before had his overwhelming advances been so lightly parried and set aside.

'Will you take a walk with me this evening after dinner?' he proposed. 'There is a most heavenly moon – and I cannot see to read to you. It must be strangely lovely – the moonlight – on your lake, is it not, Mrs Osgood?'

'It is indeed,' she warmly agreed, looking disapprovingly on the girl, who was still giggling softly at the memory of golden-haired Araminta. 'Take him on the cliff walk, Ellen, and do try to be more appreciative of beauty!'

'Yes, mama,' said Ellen, 'I'll be good.'

She was so good upon the moonlit walk; so gentle and sympathetic, and so honestly tried to find some point of agreement, that his feelings were too much for his judgment, and he seized her hand and kissed it. She pushed him away, too astonished for words.

'Why, Mr Pendexter! What are you thinking of!'

Then he poured out his heart to her. He told her how he loved her – madly, passionately, irresistably. He begged her to listen to him.

'Ah! You young Diana! You do not know how I suffer! You are so young, so cold! So heavenly beautiful! Do not be cruel! Listen to me! Say you will be my wife! Give me one kiss! Just one!'

She was young, and cold, and ignorantly cruel. She laughed at him, laughed mercilessly, and turned away.

He followed her, the blood pounding in his veins, his voice shaken with the intensity of his emotions. He caught her hand and drew her toward him again. She broke from him with a little cry, and ran. He followed, hotly, madly; rushed upon her, caught her, held her fast.

'You shall love me! You shall!' he cried. His hands were hot and trembling, but he held her close and turned her face to his.

'I will not!' she cried, struggling. 'Let me go! I hate you, I tell you. I hate you! You are – disgusting!' She pushed as far from him as he could.

They had reached the top of the little cliff opposite the

house. Huge dark pines hung over them, their wide boughs swaying softly.

The water lay below in the shadow, smooth and oil-black.

The girl looked down at it, and a sudden shudder shook her tense frame. She gave a low moan and hid her face in her hands.

'Ah!' he cried. 'It is your fate! Our fate! We have lived through this before! We will die together if we cannot live together!'

He caught her to him, kissed her madly, passionately, and together they went down into the black water.

'It's pretty lucky I could swim,' said Ellen, as she hurried home. 'And he couldn't. The poor man! O, the poor man! He must have been crazy!'